The fairy tales and rhymes in this book first appeared in *Nursery Stories, Nursery Rhymes, Hans Christian Andersen Stories* and *A Treasury of Rhymes*, all written and illustrated by Rene Cloke.

ISBN 0-86163-064-5

Published by Award Publications Ltd, London
© 1978 Award Publications Ltd
Reprinted 1984
Printed in Hungary

RENE CLOKE'S
Bedtime Book
OF FAIRYTALES AND RHYMES

AWARD PUBLICATIONS — LONDON.

Nursery

Rhymes

Curly locks, Curly locks,
Wilt thou be mine?
Thou shalt not wash dishes,
Nor yet feed the swine;
But sit on a cushion
and sew a fine seam,
And feed upon
strawberries,
sugar and
cream!

The Robin and the Wren
Fought about the porridge-pan;
And ere the Robin got a spoon,
The Wren had ate the porridge
down.

Bow! wow! wow!
Whose dog art thou?
I'm little Tommy Tinker's dog,
Bow! wow! wow!

Monday's child is fair of face,

Tuesday's child is full of grace,

Wednesday's child is full of woe,

Friday's child is loving and giving,

Thursday's child has far to go,

Saturday's child works hard for a living;

But the child that is born on the Sabbath day
Is bonny and blithe and good and gay.

5

Hark, hark! the dogs do bark,
The beggars are coming to town;
Some in rags
and some in jags,
And some in velvet gowns.

Handy Pandy, Jack-a-Dandy,
   Loved plum cake and sugar candy;
He bought some at a baker's shop,
   And then he came out,
hop, hop, hop!

There was a little girl who had a little curl
   Right in the middle of her forehead;
When she was good, she was very, very good,
   But when she was bad she was horrid.

PRIVATE
NO FISHING

Little Tommy Tittlemouse
   Lived in a little house;
He caught fishes in other men's ditches.

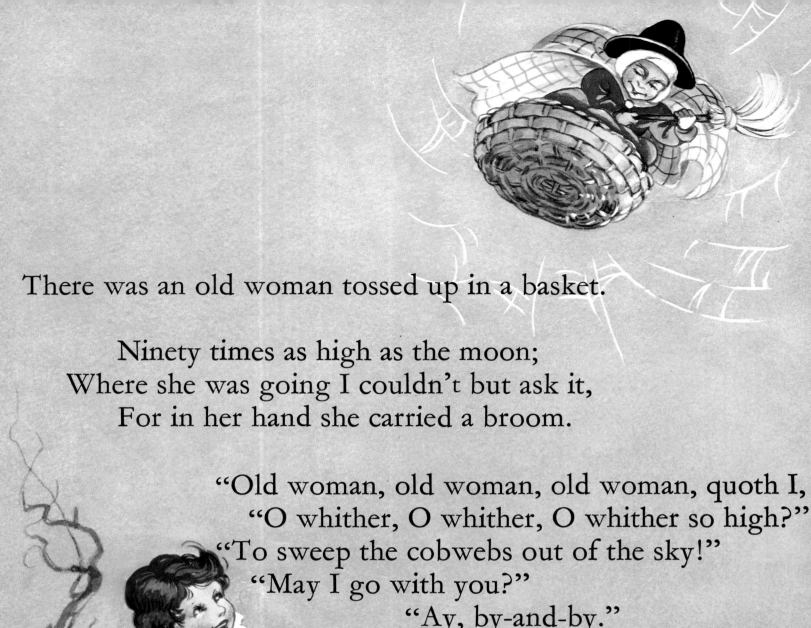

There was an old woman tossed up in a basket.

Ninety times as high as the moon;
Where she was going I couldn't but ask it,
For in her hand she carried a broom.

"Old woman, old woman, old woman, quoth I,
"O whither, O whither, O whither so high?"
"To sweep the cobwebs out of the sky!"
"May I go with you?"
                    "Ay, by-and-by."

"How many miles to Babylon?"
    "Three score miles and ten."
"Can I get there by candle-light?"
    "Yes and back again!

If your heels are nimble and light,
You may get there by candle-light."

They that wash on Monday
    Have all the week to dry;
They that wash on Tuesday
    Are not so much awry;
They that wash on Wednesday
    Are not so much to blame;
They that wash on Thursday
    Wash for shame;
They that wash on Friday
    Wash in need;
They that wash on Saturday,
    Oh, they're slow
indeed!

Wynken, Blynken and Nod one night
    Sailed off in a wooden shoe,
Sailed on a river of crystal light
    Into a sea of dew.
"Where are you going and what do you wish?"
    The old moon asked the three.
"We have come to fish for the herring fish
    That live in this beautiful sea;
Nets of silver and gold have we,"
    Said Wynken, Blynken and Nod.

The old moon laughed and sang a song,
  As they rocked in the wooden shoe;
And the wind that sped them all night long
  Ruffled the waves of dew.
The little stars were the herring fish
  That lived in that beautiful sea—
"Now cast your nets wherever you wish,—
  Never afeard are we!"
So cried the stars to the fishermen three,
  Wynken, Blynken and Nod.

Wynken and Blynken are two little eyes,
  And Nod is a little head,
And the wooden shoe that sailed the skies
  Is a wee one's trundle bed;
So shut your eyes while Mother sings
  Of the wonderful sights that be,
And you shall see the beautiful things
  As you rock in the misty sea,
Where the old shoe rocks the fishermen three,
  Wynken, Blynken and Nod.

January brings the snow,
Makes our feet and fingers glow.

February brings the rain,
Thaws the frozen lake
again.

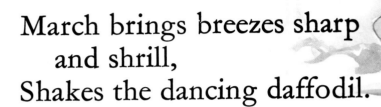

March brings breezes sharp
and shrill,
Shakes the dancing daffodil.

April brings the primrose
sweet,
Scatters daisies at our feet.

May brings flocks of pretty lambs,
Skipping by their fleecy dams.

June brings tulips,
lilies, roses,

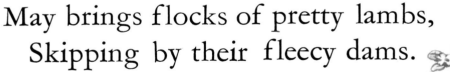
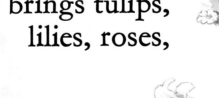

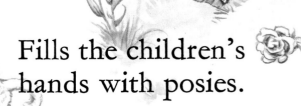

Fills the children's
hands with posies.

12

Hot July brings cooling showers,
Apricots and gillyflowers.

August brings
the sheaves of corn,
Then the harvest home is borne.

Warm September
brings the fruit
Sportsmen then
begin to shoot.

Brown October brings the pheasant,
Then to gather nuts is pleasant.

Dull November brings the blast,
Then the leaves go whirling past.

Chill December brings the sleet,
Blazing fire and Christmas treat.

I saw a ship a-sailing,
    A-sailing on the sea;
And, oh! it was all laden
    With pretty things for thee!
There were comfits in the cabin,
    And apples in the hold;

The sail was made of silk
    And the mast was made of gold.
The four-and-twenty sailors
    Who stood between the decks,
Were four-and-twenty white mice
    With chains about their necks.
The captain was a duck,
    With a packet on his back;
And when the ship began to move,
    The captain said, "Quack! quack!"

I had a little hen, the prettiest ever seen,
She washed me the dishes and kept
the house clean.

She went to the mill
to fetch me some flour,
She brought it home
in less than an hour.

She baked me my **bread,**
she brewed me my **ale,**

She sat by the fire
and told many a tale.

Lavender's blue, diddle diddle, lavender's green,
When I am king, diddle diddle, you shall be queen.

Bat, bat, come under my hat,
And I'll give you a slice of bacon;
And when I bake
I'll give you a cake,
If I am not mistaken.

One misty, moisty morning
When cloudy was the
weather;
There I met an old man
Clothed all in leather;
Clothed all in leather,
With a cap beneath
his chin,-
How do you do,
and how do you do,
And how do you do again!

Rain on the green grass,
Rain on the tree,
Rain on the house-top
But not upon me!

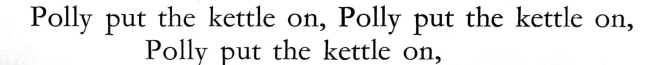

Polly put the kettle on, Polly put the kettle on,
Polly put the kettle on,
We'll all have tea.

Sukey take it off again,
Sukey take it off again,
Sukey take it off again,
They've all gone away.

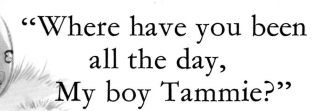

"Where have you been
all the day,
My boy Tammie?"

"I've been all the day
Courting of a lady gay;
But, oh! she's too young
To be taken from her mammy."

"She can brew and she can bake,
And she can make our wedding cake;
But, oh! she's too young
To be taken from her mammy."

Jack and Jill went up the hill
To fetch a pail of water;

Jack fell down
and broke his crown,
And Jill came tumbling after.

A frog he would a-wooing go,
Heigh-ho! says Rowley,
Whether his mother would let him or no.
With a rowley, poley,
gammon and spinach,
Heigh-ho! says Anthony Rowley.

Nursery & Woodland Stories

BY RENE CLOKE

THE RED UMBRELLA

"I think I will have a picnic by the river," said Ricky Rabbit.

He looked out of the window; the sun was shining but there were some big clouds in the sky.

"Perhaps I had better take my umbrella," he said, "it might rain and I <u>don't</u> like getting wet."

He put on his scarf, packed a flask of tea and a bag of biscuits, then he picked a big lettuce from the garden.

On the way to the river he called at the baker's shop and bought some currant buns and jam tarts.

"My little Dan and Daisy went down to the river this morning," said Mr Harvest Mouse, the baker, "and they haven't come home yet. Look out for them, will you?"

"I will," answered Ricky. "Now, tell me, do you think it will rain?"

"Oh, no!" laughed Mr Harvest Mouse, "it's a lovely day!"

"Rather a pity I brought my umbrella," thought Ricky.

The first person he met as he walked through the woods to the river was Hopscotch, the frog.

Hopscotch was feeling very cross.

"I want to take home some blackberries," he grumbled, "but they are all growing so high up that I can't reach them, fine hopper though I am."

Ricky hooked his umbrella over a branch and pulled it down.

"Oh, thank you!" cried Hopscotch, as he filled his cans, "that's splendid. I shall have enough to make bramble jelly and I will give you a pot to put in your store cupboard."

"That's very kind of you," said Ricky, "I'm fond of bramble jelly."

Ricky hummed a little tune as he walked on through the woods but he had rather a fright when he saw old Foxy taking a short cut to his den over the hill. Ricky and Foxy were not good friends and Foxy had a very hungry look in his eyes today.

"I mustn't let him see me," said Ricky and he looked around for a good hiding place.

Some big red toadstools were growing nearby, so Ricky put up his umbrella and popped underneath it.

Old Foxy thought that the red umbrella was another toadstool and went on his way without noticing the little rabbit.

"That was lucky," whispered Ricky.

He skipped along by the river looking for a comfortable place to have his tea and talking to some of the birds and animals he met.

Then he heard a little cry –
"Help! help!"

"Who is that?" called Ricky looking across the water.

There, on the grassy island in the middle of the river, Ricky saw Dan and Daisy, the two little harvest mice.

"We rowed our boat up the river and landed on this island," cried Dan.

"But the boat drifted away," sobbed Daisy, "and we can't get back."

"This looks like another job for my umbrella," decided Ricky.

He opened the big umbrella and floated it on the water, then he stepped inside and paddled out to the island.

23

"Oh, Ricky, you are clever," cried Dan, as he and Daisy scrambled in and Ricky paddled the umbrella back to the bank.

"Your umbrella makes a lovely boat," said Daisy.

"You must be hungry," said Ricky, when they were all safely ashore, "there's plenty in my basket for you both to share."

Everyone enjoyed the picnic; the lettuce and biscuits were fresh and crisp and the buns and tarts were delicious.

"Although it didn't rain," said Ricky, "it's very lucky that I took my umbrella."

BOB-A-CAT

Bob-a-Cat helped himself to marmalade and said –
"I'm going shopping to-day."
"What are you going to buy?" asked Dickory.
"Ah," replied Bob-a-Cat, mysteriously, "that's a secret."
Dickory thought this sounded most exciting, especially
as the next day was his birthday and he couldn't help
wondering if the secret might be something for him.
He pretended not to be interested and just said –
"Don't eat all the marmalade, I haven't finished my
toast."
After breakfast Bob-a-Cat took his purse from his
drawer; he knew exactly how much he had – seventy-five
pence, enough to buy a nice birthday present.
He popped his head round the kitchen door.
"I'm off, Dic," he called.
Dickory was reading a cookery book and waved his
hand without looking up. Bob-a-Cat had made him a
birthday cake but he thought he would make some jam
tarts and buns as well for his birthday party tomorrow.

Bob-a-Cat tried to think of the
best kind of birthday present
for Dickory.
"He has a bat and ball and a
bucket and spade, I must think
of something quite new."
He crossed the river by
the little bridge and
thought about boats, but
Dickory already had two.
He met Barbara Bunny
riding her bicycle.
"I'd like to buy Dickory
a bicycle," thought
Bob-a-Cat, "but I'm
afraid they cost more
than seventy-five pence."

When he reached the market, he found that the stalls were full of such wonderful things that he was quite bewildered.

"I won't buy sweets or chocolates," he decided, "I might want to eat them myself."

He saw some gay hats on another stall.

"But I don't know what size to get," said Bob-a-Cat, "and a hat that didn't fit would be a silly sort of present."

The next stall was the best; there were garden tools and watering-cans and little wheelbarrows, red, green and blue.

"Dickory would like a wheelbarrow for the garden better than anything," sighed Bob-a-Cat, "but, oh dear, they're ninety pence and I've only seventy-five."

27

He wandered round the market looking at saucepans and brushes and other unbirthday kind of things and, at last, he went back to the stall with the wheelbarrows.

"Trying to make up your mind which colour to have?" asked old Badger, the stall keeper.

"They're all beautiful," said Bob-a-Cat, "but I haven't got ninety pence, have you – have you – just one that's cheaper?"

"Well, as a matter of fact, I have," said the stall keeper, "this one is a bit scratched; I was going to touch it up with some red paint –

90ᴾ

– but I'll let you have it for seventy-five pence." "Oh, thank you!" gasped Bob-a-Cat, "it's a lovely one!" He paid old Badger and trundled off with the wheelbarrow.

When Bob-a-Cat got home he crept around to the back of the house and pushed the wheelbarrow into the garden shed.

He painted over the scratches with red paint and it looked as good as new, then he hid it behind a box and tip-toed along to the front door.

"Hullo," said Dickory, "did you get your secret?"

"Wait and see," laughed Bob-a-Cat. He wasn't carrying anything except his empty purse; it was all very exciting and mysterious.

Bob-a-Cat had a glass of milk for supper and Dickory had some cocoa; they ate two broken jam tarts which were not good enough for the party.

When Bob-a-Cat awoke the next morning, Dickory was still asleep.

"I'll put the wheelbarrow beside the breakfast table," whispered Bob-a-Cat as he hurried downstairs and out into the garden.

It was a beautiful morning, the sun was shining and the flowers were nodding in a very birthdayish kind of way.

Bob-a-Cat looked inside the shed – he looked behind the box – the wheelbarrow –

WASN'T THERE!

He peered here and there and everywhere, what could have happened to it?

"It's gone – it's gone!" he cried, running back to the house, "my wonderful secret present has gone!"

"What _is_ the matter?" asked Dickory, "have you lost something?"

"It's your birthday present," sobbed Bob-a-Cat, "I hid it in the shed and now it's gone!"

Dickory helped him to search but, of course, he didn't know what to look for.

"It's big and red," said Bob-a-Cat, "but I can't tell you what it is because it's a secret."

"Hullo," called Mr Ottery, the postman, "I knocked at your door an hour ago but you must have been asleep.

I had so many letters and parcels for Dickory that I took a little wheelbarrow from your shed to put them in; you'll find them in the front porch."

Bob-a-Cat flew round the house and, there in the porch, was the wheelbarrow full of presents.

"It's the most wonderful secret present I've ever had!" gasped Dickory.

"Happy Birthday!" shouted Bob-a-Cat.

"Happy Birthday!" laughed the postman, "and don't oversleep next time!"

SILLY SQUIRRELS

Some squirrels are very silly; they can't see further than the end of their noses. If they could see as far as the end of their bushy tails they would be very wise indeed.

"Let's do something special for Christmas," said Bilberry.

"Let's not wash up," suggested Candytuft. "That's a good idea," said Bilberry, "it's Christmas Eve tomorrow, we won't wash up for three days.

Nothing could be more special than not washing up."

Bilberry and Candytuft had a lovely time on the next day; they hung paper chains and balloons all over the house and hung a garland of holly on the front door, they made a snowman and they went sliding on the pond.

They didn't wash up the breakfast dishes or the mid-morning drinks or the lunch; by the time they had finished tea there were stacks and stacks of plates and cups and saucers as well as knives and forks and spoons in the kitchen.

You wouldn't think that two squirrels could use so many dishes.

It was getting cold and dark so Bilberry took his lantern and they both looked out for the postman.

"Some letters and parcels for you both," cried Mr Rabbity, "and a telegram."

"Who can this be from?" said Bilberry as he tore it open. "EXPECT US BOTH FOR CHRISTMAS DAY LOVE UNCLE FUZZ AND AUNT BUSHY."

Bilberry and Candytuft were delighted. They went back to the kitchen, but, oh dear! There was the pile of dishes waiting to be washed and nothing clean for a Christmas Day party.

"This will take us all night," declared Candytuft seizing a bowl and turning the tap. But there was no water.

"The pipes have frozen," moaned Bilberry, "now what shall we do?"

"Get a bucket of snow and melt it on the fire," said Candytuft.

They were tired out by bedtime and Bilberry said he would rather go to bed without any supper than fetch more snow to wash up the plates afterwards.

The next morning they were both up early.

"Hurray!" cried Bilberry, "the thaw has come and the taps are running!"

Candytuft made some mince pies, Bilberry polished the spoons and forks and the table was set with the nice clean china just as Uncle Fuzz and Aunt Bushy drove up to the door.

"Merry Christmas!" called out Aunt Bushy, "I've brought you a Christmas cake for tea."

"Merry Christmas!" shouted Uncle Fuzz as he struggled to get a huge package from his car. "Here's a present that I think you'll find really useful!"

And what do you think it was?

A DISHWASHER

FAWNS IN FANCY DRESS

"The first of March!" cried Bracken the fawn, "the day of Mrs Badger's fancy dress party!"

His sister Catkin picked up the pair of fairy wings she had made the night before.

"I shall be the Spring Fairy at the party," she said. "Let's go to the woods this afternoon and gather flowers for a garland for my head."

"Good idea," answered Bracken, "I might find some more feathers for my head-dress; I'm going to be a Red Indian, we shall look a very fine pair!"

Catkin put a bottle of milk and some biscuits in a basket while Bracken painted some of the feathers on his head-dress with red and blue paint.

They trotted through the wood talking of all the fun they would have at the party that night.

"There are some primroses and a few violets," said Catkin, "I must have those."

Bracken picked a twig of hazel catkins and a bunch of periwinkles and put them in the basket with the other flowers.

After they had had their milk and biscuits and a friendly pigeon had given Bracken two loose feathers, the fawns decided to go home, but then everything began to go wrong.

Catkin saw some early kingcups growing at the edge of the river.

"Those are just what I want," she cried and galloped down to the water. The kingcups were difficult to pick and Catkin stretched too far and tumbled into the river.

Bracken helped her out and rubbed her dry.

"We'll take a short cut along this path," he said, "we mustn't be late for the party."

But the short cut was a very long one; the path turned this way and that until it grew dark and the fawns were not sure which way they were going.

"Come on," said Bracken, "through these bushes, this *must* be the way" and he bounded off.

The next moment, with a yell of terror, he disappeared. "Where are you?" screamed Catkin dashing after him and, before she could stop herself, she fell – slither, slither – down, down – bump! into a deep pit where Bracken was sitting rubbing his head.

"We shall never be able to get out of this pit," groaned Catkin.

"People in a book send a message in a bottle," said Bracken, "just throw it in the sea for someone to pick up – well, we've got a bottle!"

"But no pencil and paper," said Catkin, "and there's no sea."

Bracken thought for a moment, then he took the twig of hazel catkins from the basket and picked a piece of nearby bracken.

"I'll put these into the milk bottle," he said, "and throw it out of the pit; if anyone picks it up in the morning they'll say 'Catkin and Bracken' and look for us!"

He threw the bottle as far as he could out of the pit.

"I hope that lands on the path – it's a plastic bottle and won't break," then Bracken lay down and put his head on his knees, "I'm afraid we've missed the party" he sighed, "so we had better go to sleep."

It was morning when a cheerful voice awakened them.

"Hullo! what are you two doing down there?"

Mr Badger's face peeped over the edge of the pit.

"Just a moment, I've got a ladder in my van, I'll have you out in a jiffy."

Before long, Bracken and Catkin were scrambling up the ladder and out of the pit.

"Lucky I came this way," said Mr Badger, "I saw that bottle lying on the path and stopped to pick it up; 'Bracken and Catkin' I says, says I, those two fawns must be somewhere about and in trouble and right I was! A very clever idea of yours!"

They all clambered into Mr Badger's van.

"I drove to the wood with my ladder to gather greenery for our fancy dress party tonight," continued Mr Badger.

"Tonight?" cried Bracken and Catkin, "but yesterday was the first of March and we missed the party!"

"Ha! ha!" laughed the badger, "don't you know the old rhyme about the days of February?

'Twenty-eight are all its score,
Except in Leap Year, once in four,
February's days are one day more.'

This year is Leap Year, yesterday was the twenty-ninth of February and today's the first of March!"

"Hurray! Primroses and violets, I'll be the Spring Fairy after all!"

"Bows and arrows and tomahawks!" yelled Bracken, "and I'll be the Indian Chief!"

PAINT AND PEPPERMINT

Jeremy Squirrel walked from his cottage down to
the river where his little boat lay in the rushes.

It was a bright autumn day and the leaves were
floating down from the willow trees; a sharp wind sent ripples
over the water and Jeremy gave a shiver.

"Winter is coming," he said, "and my boat is looking shabby;
I will buy a tin of paint, light blue, I think, and paint her
ready for the spring. I shall be sleeping most of the winter
and I shan't want to row on the river."

He pushed his boat into the water, hopped in and took the oars.

"I'll go up the river to old Vole's shop and choose the paint,"
he decided.

There was great excitement in the little shop and old Vole
looked very annoyed.

"Some young villain stole into my shop last night," he told Jeremy, "and took packets of chocolate, sticks of peppermint rock and bars of candy. He can't have been a very big animal, he left such small footmarks."

"I'll help you to keep a sharp look out for the thief," said Jeremy as he chose a tin of forget-me-not blue for his boat and white paint for the inside.

Spindle Hedgehog was sitting outside the shop and Jeremy, turning to speak to him as he stepped into his boat, slipped and went splash! into the water.

He was able to scramble back into his boat but he had quite a search for one of the tins of paint; at last his boat-hook caught round a handle and he was able to pull the tin from amongst the rushes.

He hung his wet shirt on the oar to dry; it made quite a good sail and Jeremy was feeling happy again by the time he reached home.

"I'll start painting at once," he decided and opened the tin of blue paint.

"What's this?" he spluttered in amazement.

Instead of blue paint, the tin held a red spotted scarf full of chocolate, sticks of peppermint rock and candy!

Jeremy dashed down to the river and pushed off in his boat.

"This will be a surprise for old Vole!"

And it was.

"After putting the stolen sweets in an empty paint tin, the thief must have heard someone coming," said the shopkeeper, "and dropped the tin in the rushes –"

"– planning to come for it later on," finished Jeremy.

"If I'm not mistaken, that scarf belongs to young Sid Shrew," said old Vole.

"Let's wait by the river tonight and catch him," suggested Jeremy, "he will find my tin of paint and think it is the one he hid."

So when it was dark the two animals hid by the waterside and, before long, a small figure crept by the river path; he began poking about amongst the rushes and gave a squeak of satisfaction as he pulled out a paint tin.

But when he opened it, he cried out in surprise.

"Not quite what you expected to find?" asked old Vole, seizing him by the collar.

Little Sid Shrew was so frightened and so surprised and puzzled and he begged so very hard to be forgiven that old Vole gave him a good lecture and let him go.

The next day Jeremy received a present and the label said –
"Dear Jeremy,
Thank you for your help. Here is a red sail for your boat, a better one than a wet shirt!
Yours Old Vole."

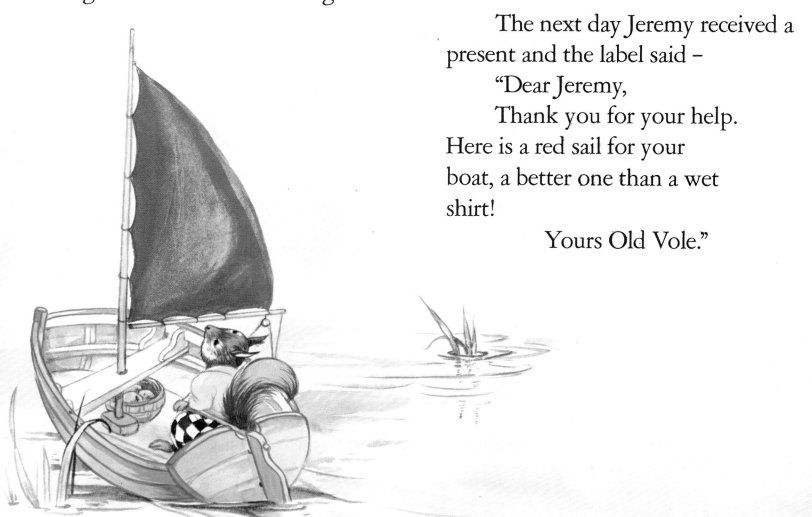

PANCAKE DAY

"Bill!" cried Mrs Bobbity, "will you chop some wood for the fire, I have just finished making the carrot soup and I must go down to the market garden to get tomatoes for the salad."

Mr Bobbity looked up from his book.

"You're getting lunch ready rather early," he grumbled, "Aunt Fluffypaws won't be here yet."

"I have to mix the batter for the pancakes," answered Mrs Bobbity, tying on her bonnet, "I shall be ready only just in time."

Mr Bobbity wandered into the garden taking his book with him; it was a very exciting story and he *had* to read a few more pages before he started work.

At last the chapter was finished.

"It's getting rather late," cried Mr Bobbity and, seizing his chopper, he chopped a bundle of wood and hurried into the kitchen.

He lighted the fire and put the saucepan of soup to start cooking while he began to read the next chapter of his book.

The story became more and more exciting, the soup became hotter and hotter and at last – bubble – bubble – it boiled all over the kitchen floor!

"Horrors!" gasped Mr Bobbity.

He mopped up the floor and re-lit the fire, then he looked at the drop of soup left in the saucepan.

"Only one thing to do," he muttered, so, putting on his jacket, he hurried to the little shop next door.

He bought a large tin of carrot and parsley soup and, hiding this under his jacket, he ran home.

When Mrs Bobbity came back there was a good fire in the kitchen and the saucepan of soup waiting to be cooked.

"You stir the soup while I mix the pancake batter," she told Mr Bobbity, "and we'll soon be ready."

Mr Bobbity watched her tossing the pancakes and thought what fun it must be
"Let me toss just one!" he begged.

But it wasn't as easy as it looked and he tossed the pancake so
high that it stuck to the ceiling.

"How stupid you are!" scolded Mrs Bobbity, "we can't get that down
without borrowing a ladder – well, perhaps it won't show stuck to the
rafter. You will have to be the one to go without a second helping."

She had just finished cooking the rest of the pancakes when Aunt
Fluffypaws arrived and they all sat down to lunch.

Mrs Bobbity looked hard at the soup.

"Parsley?" she murmured, "I never put parsley in my carrot soup, what can have happened to it?"

Mr Bobbity didn't notice it, he was too busy watching the pancake coming unstuck from the ceiling and then – plop – it fell lightly on Aunt Fluffypaws' hat.

Mr and Mrs Bobbity looked at each other, what *should* they do?

Mrs Bobbity tried to pick it off when she fetched the salad but Aunt Fluffypaws moved her head and she missed it. Mr Bobbity tried to pull it off when he brought the dish of pancakes to the table but it was stuck fast to a bunch of flowers on the side of the hat.

After lunch, Mr Bobbity said that he would walk home with Aunt Fluffypaws and Mrs Bobbity whispered.

"You *must* get that pancake off her hat before she sees it!"

Ten minutes later, Mr Bobbity burst into the kitchen.

"All's well!" he cried, "as we walked along the lane, dozens of birds came fluttering down and before you could say 'Winkypop' they'd pecked all the pancake off Aunt Fluffypaws' hat! She was so interested in the exciting story I was telling her that she didn't notice what was happening."

Mrs Bobbity gave a sigh of relief.

"But I'm still puzzled about that soup," she said, "it certainly didn't taste like my usual carrot soup and I know I didn't put in any parsley."

Mr Bobbity crept out into the garden; he cut up the empty soup tin into little pieces and threaded them on a string to keep the birds off his lettuces.

Then *he* gave a sigh of relief.

"No need for anyone to know about that," he said.

Hans Andersen Fairy Tales

THUMBELINA

A young wife was talking one day to a wise old woman who was really a fairy.

"Oh, I do wish I had a little child of my own," she sighed.

"Take this barley corn," said the wise woman, "sow it in a plant pot and you shall see what you shall see!"

"Thank you," said the young wife and she went home and put the barley corn in a pot, just as the wise woman had told her.

Almost at once a plant began to grow.

It became taller and taller and, at last, a beautiful bud appeared.

"What a lovely flower", cried the young woman and she kissed the folded petals.

Then the flower opened and there in the centre sat a tiny little girl.

The woman was delighted.

"I will call her Thumbelina," she decided, "for she is scarcely taller than my thumb. I will make her a cradle from a walnut shell with flower petals for sheets."

One night when Thumbelina was asleep, an old toad hopped through the window.

"This pretty little girl would make a good wife for my son," she croaked and, taking the walnut shell cradle, she crawled back to the stream where she lived with her ugly son.

"We will leave her on this water lily leaf," said the mother toad, "while we decorate our home with kingcups and bullrushes."

Poor Thumbelina sat on the broad leaf and cried so bitterly that a kind fish gnawed through the stem of the leaf and Thumbelina floated away down the stream where the toads could not follow her.

A white butterfly fluttered by and Thumbelina tied her sash around him and on and on they went together; then a cockchafer picked her up, flew away with her and left her sitting on a daisy.

All through the summer Thumbelina lived in the woods but when the winter came there was no shelter for her and she grew so cold that she had to wrap herself in a leaf.

One evening she came to the house of a field mouse at the edge of a corn field and begged a little corn to eat.

"Come in," cried the mouse, "and warm yourself, you poor little thing!"

The field mouse was very kind.

"You may live in my house all the winter," she said, "you can help me to keep it clean and tell me stories; I love to listen to stories."

They lived together very comfortably.

"We are to have a visitor soon," the mouse told Thumbelina one day, "my neighbour, the mole, is calling to see me. He would be a fine husband for you, for his house is much bigger than mine."

But Thumbelina did not like the old mole; he had never seen the sun or the flowers and lived all his life underground.

He told them about a dead bird which lay in one of his tunnels.

"He is a silly swallow who sang and chirped throughout the summer," grumbled the mole, "and now he is starved and frozen."

Thumbelina felt so sorry for the poor bird that she crept out of her bed that night and took a little rug to spread over him.

"Thank you for your songs, dear bird," she whispered and kissed him gently.

To her surprise she found that the bird was not dead after all and soon revived with the warmth of the rug.

Every day she brought him food and water but she didn't tell the mole and the field mouse that he was alive.

The bird soon grew stronger and when the spring came he said good-bye to Thumbelina.

"Fly on my back to the green
countryside," he begged her.

"No," said Thumbelina sadly, "the
field mouse will be very vexed if I
leave her, so good-bye, dear bird,
good-bye," and she went back to
the little house.

"We must make some pretty clothes for your wedding," said
the field mouse, "for you are to marry dear old mole in
the autumn."

In the evenings, the mole would listen to Thumbelina's
stories, while the field mouse sewed beautiful little dresses
for the wedding.

When the autumn came, Thumbelina begged the field mouse
to let her wander once more in the fields before she had to
live underground.

"Run along, then," said the field mouse kindly, "but don't wander too far."

Thumbelina looked at the blue sky and felt the sun warming her face.

"Tweet – tweet."

There was a fluttering of wings and the swallow flew over her head.

"The winter will soon be here," he chirped, "come with me and I will take you to warm countries away from the old mole and his dark house full of tunnels! You saved my life, now let me help you."

"Yes, yes!" cried Thumbelina and she scrambled on to the swallow's back.

Away they went, over the sea and over snowy mountains, until they came to a land where the sun shone more brightly than Thumbelina had ever seen it.

The swallow came to rest on an old marble pillar in a lovely garden by the side of a lake and Thumbelina looked around in delight.

In a beautiful white flower stood an elf wearing a golden crown. "I am the king of the fairies," he told Thumbelina, "will you be my queen?"

So Thumbelina became the queen of the fairies and was given many presents; the best of all was a pair of butterfly wings so that she and the fairy king could fly together from flower to flower for evermore.

THE PRINCESS AND THE SWINEHERD

There was once a Prince who wished to marry a Princess but he was not rich and all he could give her was a rose and a nightingale.

He sent these to the palace in fine caskets and the Princess clapped her hands in great excitement.

"I wonder if one holds a kitten and the other a musical box," she cried.

But when she saw the rose and the nightingale she was disappointed.

"They are both real," she complained, "I wish they were toy ones."

The Prince, however, was not discouraged; he dressed himself in old clothes and asked for work at the palace.

"Well," said the King, "I do need someone to look after the pigs."

So the Prince became the Royal Swineherd.

He sat in the pigsty and worked away making a little cooking pot with bells on it.

When it boiled, it played a merry tune
and anyone who put his finger in the steam
could smell just what everyone in the town was
having for dinner.

The Princess heard the tune and longed to have the cooking
pot, so her Maid of Honour asked the Swineheard the price of it.
"I want ten kisses from the Princess," the Swineheard told her.
"How tiresome!" said the Princess, "but I must have it. All my
ladies must spread their skirts so that no one can see me."

So the Swineheard got the ten kisses and the Princess and her
ladies had a merry time with the little cooking pot.

The next thing the Swineheard made was a
rattle which played all the tunes in the world.

"How much does he want for it?"
asked the Princess.

"One hundred kisses," answered
the Maid of Honour.

The ladies held out their skirts to hide the Princess but this time the King was looking out of his window.

"You rascals!" he cried. "Off you go, both of you!"

So the Princess and the Swineherd were banished from the palace.

"I wish I had married the Prince who sent me the rose and the nightingale." sobbed the Princess.

The Swineherd threw off his rough clothes and appeared in his princely costume.

"You would not accept a Prince who was poor," he cried, "but you would give your kisses to a Swineherd for a silly toy. Now, I despise you."

He went back to his own kingdom and shut his palace door and the Princess was left crying in the rain.

THE SHEPHERDESS AND THE CHIMNEY-SWEEP

Two little china figures stood on a table and looked at each other; one was a Shepherdess and one was a Chimney Sweep.

"How beautiful she is," sighed the Chimney Sweep, "her face is so pink and white and her dress is so graceful."

"Although he is a Chimney Sweep," said the Shepherdess, "he is as clean and neat as a Prince."

They loved each other very much and would have been quite happy if it had not been for the Field-Marshal-Major-General-Corporal-Sergeant.

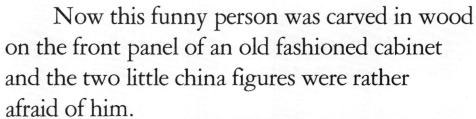

Now this funny person was carved in wood on the front panel of an old fashioned cabinet and the two little china figures were rather afraid of him.

The Chinese Mandarin, who was the grandfather of the Shepherdess, nodded his head. "He will make you a fine husband, he has a whole cabinet of silver!"

"I won't marry him!" declared the Shepherdess, "I don't want to live in a gloomy cabinet."

The Chimney Sweep comforted her.

"We will creep off this table," he whispered, "and go into the wide world. I will work for you, sweeping chimneys."

When the Chinese Mandarin was asleep, they stepped down from the table and ran across the floor.

First they hid in an open drawer where some playing cards were watching a puppet theatre, but the play was very sad and made the Shepherdess cry, so they had to find another hiding place.

"We had better climb up the chimney," said the Chimney Sweep, "that will lead us out to the wide world. I know the way – are you brave enough to come with me?"

"Yes," whispered the Shepherdess.

The Chinese Mandarin woke up and started rocking his head to and fro.

"Quick!" cried the Chimney Sweep, and, taking the Shepherdess by the hand, he hurried to the fireplace.

It was very dark in the chimney but they could see a star shining down through the chimney-pot as they climbed slowly up and up.

At last they reached the roof and sat down to rest, for they were very tired.

The sky above them was full of stars and all the wide world lay beneath them.

"Oh, dear," cried the little Shepherdess, "I'm frightened, the world is too big! I wish I were back on the table again."

The Chimney Sweep reminded her of the Chinese Mandarin and the old Field-Marshal-Major-General-Corporal-Sergeant, but she wept so much that he had to agree to take her back again.

Down the chimney they crept, to the fireplace and into the room.

There, on the floor, lay the Chinese Mandarin broken in pieces, for he had fallen off the table when he had tried to follow the runaways.

"Poor Grandfather, I wonder if he can be mended?" said the Shepherdess.

He *was* mended but a stiff rivet was put in his neck and he could no longer nod his head to and fro.

"Can I have your grand-daughter for my wife?" asked the Field-Marshal-Major-General-Corporal-Sergeant, but the Chinese Mandarin couldn't nod his head, so the two little china figures remained together on the table and loved each other for ever and ever.

THE UGLY DUCKLING

A mother duck sat on her eggs in a nest by the river and hoped that they would soon hatch for she had been there a long time and was getting tired.

Crack! crack! one day the shells broke and eight yellow ducklings appeared.

"How pretty they are!" declared a friend who was visiting her, "but there is still one more to hatch; what a large egg it is; I hope

it's not a turkey egg, I was once deceived by one."

"I will sit on it a little longer," decided the mother duck, "it may be a particularly fine bird."

She sat on it all day and at last it cracked and out came a large ugly duckling.

"Well, he's certainly the largest of them all," said the mother duck, "now I had better take them all back to the farm."
"He must be a young turkey!" declared the other birds in the farmyard but, no, the ugly one could swim as well as the others.

Everyone was very unkind to the poor duckling and at last he decided to run away.

He spent the night with some wild ducks but the next morning a shooting party came to the marsh, bang! bang! went the guns and the duckling ran away again. That night he came to an old cottage where a poor woman lived with her cat and hen but they were not very kind to him so, feeling sad, he wandered off to a nearby pond.

The next evening a flock of beautiful white birds with long
necks flew overhead.

"How lovely they are!" sighed the duckling.

Autumn came and then winter. The water in the pond became
colder and colder and the duckling had to keep swimming to
stop it from freezing.

At last he became so tired that he lay down and let the water
freeze to ice around him.

In the morning a kind peasant came by and, taking off his
shoe, he broke the ice and rescued the duckling.

"I'll take him home for the
children to play with," said
the peasant, but the
duckling was so used to
being teased by everyone
that he was frightened
when he saw the girls and
boys looking at him.

He dashed around the kitchen, jumped into a milk pail,
then into a flour bin and the children rushed after him
shouting and laughing as they tried to catch him.
He reached the door and escaped into the snowy countryside.
The winter was long and cold and the poor little ugly duckling
sheltered amongst the bushes and was very, very miserable.
And then the spring came.

The sun shone warmly, the birds sang and the duckling
stretched his wings and found that they felt bigger and
stronger than before.
"I will fly off and find some water to swim in," he decided and
away he flew to a beautiful garden where there was a large pond.
Three lovely swans were swimming there and the duckling
looked at them sadly.

"I will ask them to kill me," he said, "much better to be killed by those handsome birds than to be hated and despised by everyone."

He flew down to the water and bowed his head–but what had happened?

Reflected in the water was no ugly duckling but a lovely white swan. The other swans swam around him and greeted him kindly and a group of children ran up to the pond.

"A new swan!" they cried, "he is the most beautiful of them all." And the new swan raised his neck and was happy at last, for he was no longer an ugly duckling.

Good-bye!